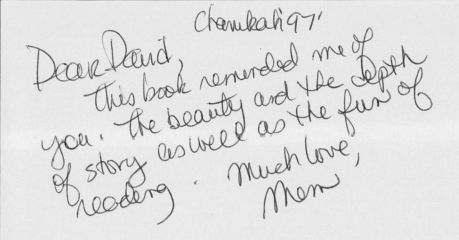

Chanukah 97'

Dear David,
   This book reminded me of
you. the beauty and the depth
of story as well as the fun of
reading. Much love,
         Mom

# The River Bank

## and Other Stories From
## THE WIND IN THE WILLOWS

*The Mole had been working hard all the morning.*

# *The* River Bank

## and *Other Stories From*
## THE WIND IN THE WILLOWS

KENNETH GRAHAME

*illustrated by*
INGA MOORE

CANDLEWICK PRESS
CAMBRIDGE, MASSACHUSETTS

*For David, Amelia & Mara*

*I. M.*

This book comprises the first five stories
of Kenneth Grahame's classic work for children
*The Wind in the Willows,* first published in 1908.
The stories have been carefully abridged by the illustrator,
who has ensured that the words almost always
remain those of the author.

Illustrations copyright © 1996 by Inga Moore

First U.S. edition 1996

Library of Congress Cataloging-in-Publication Data

Grahame, Kenneth, 1859–1932.
The river bank : and other stories from the Wind in the willows /
Kenneth Grahame ; abridged and illustrated by Inga Moore.—1st U.S. ed.
Contents: The river bank—The open road—The wild wood—Mr Badger—Dulce domum.
Summary: The escapades of four animal friends who live along a river in the English
countryside—Toad, Mole, Rat, and Badger.
ISBN 0-7636-0059-8
[1. Animals—Fiction.] I. Moore, Inga, ill. II. Grahame, Kenneth, 1859–1932.
Wind in the willows. III. Title. PZ7.G759Ri 1996 [Fic]—dc20 96-10565

2 4 6 8 10 9 7 5 3

Printed in Hong Kong

This book was typeset in M Bembo.
The pictures were done in ink and pastel crayon.

Candlewick Press
2067 Massachusetts Avenue
Cambridge, Massachusetts 02140

# Contents

## ONE

# *The River Bank*

The Mole had been working hard all the morning, spring-cleaning his little home. First with brooms, then with dusters; then on ladders and steps and chairs, with a brush and a pail of whitewash; till he had dust in his throat and eyes, and splashes of whitewash all over his black fur, and an aching back and weary arms. Spring was moving in the air above and in the earth below, around even his dark and lowly little house, and suddenly he flung down his brush, said "Bother!" and "O blow!" and also "Hang spring-cleaning!" and bolted out of the house without even waiting to put on his coat. Making for the steep tunnel which answered in his case to the gravelled drive owned by animals whose residences are nearer to the sun and air, he scraped and scratched and scrabbled and scrooged, then he scrooged again and scrabbled and scraped, muttering, "Up we go! Up we go!" till at last . . .

 pop! his snout came out into the sunlight, and he found himself rolling in the warm grass of a great meadow.

"This is fine," he said to himself. "This is better than whitewashing!"

Jumping off all his four legs at once, in the joy of living and spring without its cleaning, he pursued his way across the meadow till he reached the further side.

He rambled busily along the hedgerows, across copses, finding everywhere birds building, flowers budding, leaves thrusting.

As he meandered aimlessly along, suddenly he stood by the edge of a full-fed river. Never in his life had he seen a river before. All was a-shake and a-shiver—gleams and sparkles, chatter and bubble. The Mole was bewitched. By its side he trotted spellbound; and when tired at last, he sat on the bank.

As he sat and looked across to the bank opposite, a dark hole just above the water's edge caught his eye and dreamily he fell to considering what a snug dwelling-place it would make for an animal with few wants and fond of a bijou riverside residence, when something bright and small seemed to twinkle down in the heart of it like a tiny star. But it could hardly be a star. Then, as he looked, it winked at him, and so declared itself to be an eye; and a small face began gradually to grow up round it, like a frame round a picture.

A brown face with whiskers.

A grave round face, with a twinkle in its eye.

Small neat ears and thick silky hair.

It was the Water Rat!

"Hullo, Mole!" said the Water Rat.

"Hullo, Rat!" said the Mole.

"Would you like to come over?" inquired the Rat presently.

"O, it's all very well to *talk*!" said the Mole rather pettishly, he being new to a river and riverside life and its ways.

The Rat said nothing, but stooped and unfastened a rope and hauled on it; then lightly stepped into a little boat. It was painted blue outside and white within and was just the size for two animals; and the Mole's whole heart went out to it at once.

The Rat sculled smartly across and made fast. Then he held up his fore-paw as the Mole stepped gingerly down and, to his surprise, found himself actually seated in the stern of a real boat.

"This has been a wonderful day!" said he, as the Rat shoved off and took the sculls again. "Do you know, I've never been in a boat before in all my life."

"What?" cried the Rat, open-mouthed. "Never been in a— you never—well, I—what have you been doing, then?"

"Is it so nice as all that?" asked the Mole shyly.

"Nice? It's the *only* thing," said the Water Rat solemnly, as he leant forward for his stroke. "Believe me, my friend, there is *nothing*—absolutely nothing—half so much worth doing as simply messing about in boats. Simply messing," he went on dreamily: "messing—about—in—boats; messing—"

"Look ahead, Rat!" cried Mole suddenly.

It was too late. The boat struck the bank full tilt. The Rat lay on his back at the bottom of the boat, his heels in the air.

"—about in boats," he went on, picking himself up with a pleasant laugh. "Look here! If you've really nothing else on this morning, supposing we drop down the river together and have a long day of it?"

The Mole waggled his toes from sheer happiness, spread his chest with a sigh and leaned back blissfully into the soft cushions. "*What* a day I'm having!" he said. "Let us start at once!"

"Hold hard a minute, then!" said the Rat. He looped the painter through a ring in his landing-stage, climbed up into his hole above and reappeared staggering under a fat wicker luncheon-basket.

"Shove that under your feet," he observed to the Mole. Then he untied the painter and took the sculls again.

"What's inside it?" asked the Mole, wriggling with curiosity.

"There's cold chicken inside it," replied the Rat briefly;

"coldtonguecoldhamcoldbeefpickledgherkinssaladfrenchrolls cresssandwichespottedmeatgingerbeerlemonadesodawater—"

"O stop, stop," cried the Mole in ecstasies: "This is too much!"

"Do you really think so?" inquired the Rat seriously. "It's only what I always take and the other animals tell me I'm a mean beast and cut it *very* fine!"

The Mole never heard a word he was saying. Absorbed in the new life, the scents and the sounds and the sunlight, he trailed a paw in the water and dreamed waking dreams. The Water Rat, like the good fellow he was, sculled on.

"I like your clothes awfully, old chap," he remarked after some half hour or so. "I'm going to get a black velvet smoking-suit myself some day."

"I beg your pardon," said the Mole, pulling himself together with an effort. "You must think me very rude; but all this is so new to me. So—this—is—a—River!"

"*The* River," corrected the Rat.

"And you really live by it? What a jolly life!"

"By it and with it and on it and in it," said the Rat. "It's my world, and I don't want any other."

"But isn't it a bit dull at times?" the Mole ventured to ask. "Just you and the river, and no one else to pass a word with?"

"No one else to—well, of course," said the Rat. "You're new to it. The bank is so crowded nowadays that many people are moving away altogether. O no, it isn't what it used to be, at all. Kingfishers, dabchicks, moorhens about all day long always wanting you to *do* something."

"What lies over *there*?" asked the Mole, waving a paw towards a wood that darkly framed the water-meadows on one side.

"That? O, that's just the Wild Wood," said the Rat shortly. "We don't go there very much, we river-bankers."

"Aren't they—aren't they very *nice* people there?" said the Mole a trifle nervously.

"W-e-ll," replied the Rat, "the squirrels are all right. *And* the rabbits—some of 'em, but rabbits are a mixed lot. And then there's Badger. He lives right in the heart of it. Dear old Badger! Nobody interferes with *him*!"

"Why, who *should* interfere with him?" asked the Mole.

"Well, of course—there—are others," explained the Rat. "Weasels—and stoats—foxes—and so on. They're all right in a way, but they break out sometimes, there's no denying it and —you can't really trust them, that's the fact!"

"And beyond the Wild Wood?" asked the Mole.

"The Wide World," said the Rat. "And that doesn't matter."

Leaving the main stream, they passed into what seemed like a land-locked lake. Green turf sloped down to either edge, while ahead of them the silvery shoulder of a weir, arm-in-arm with a mill-wheel, that held up in its turn a grey-gabled mill-house, filled the air with a soothing murmur of sound.

It was so very beautiful that the Mole could only hold up both paws

and gasp, "O my! O my! O my!"

The Rat brought the boat alongside the bank, made her fast, helped the Mole ashore and swung out the luncheon-basket. The Mole begged to be allowed to unpack it all by himself. The Rat was very pleased to indulge him and to sprawl on the grass and rest while his excited friend shook out the tablecloth and spread it, took out the mysterious packets one by one and arranged their contents in due order, still gasping "O my! O my!" When all was ready, the Rat said, "Pitch in, old fellow!" and the Mole was very glad to obey, for he had started his spring-cleaning very early that morning, and had not paused for a bite since.

"What are you looking at?" asked the Rat presently, when the Mole's eyes were able to wander off the tablecloth a little.

"I am looking," said the Mole, "at a streak of bubbles travelling along the surface of the water."

"Bubbles? Oho!" said the Rat.

A broad, glistening muzzle showed itself above the bank, and the Otter hauled himself out and shook the water from his coat.

"Greedy beggars!" he observed. "Why didn't you invite me, Ratty?

"Such a rumpus everywhere!" he continued. "All the world seems out on the river today. I came up this backwater to get a moment's peace—and stumble on you fellows! At least—I beg your pardon—I don't exactly mean that."

There was a rustle behind them from a hedge, where last year's leaves still clung thick and a stripy head peered forth.

"Come on, old Badger!" shouted the Rat.

The Badger trotted forward a pace or two; then grunted "Hmm! Company," turned his back and disappeared.

"That's *just* the sort of fellow he is!" observed the disappointed Rat. "Simply hates Society! We shan't see any more of him today. Well, tell us, *who's* out on the river?"

"Toad's out, for one," replied the Otter. "In his brand-new wager-boat; new togs, new everything!"

The two animals looked at each other and laughed.

"Once, it was nothing but sailing," said the Rat. "Then he tired of that and took to punting. Last year it was house-boating, and we all had to go with him and pretend we liked it. It's all the same, whatever he takes up; he gets tired of it, and starts on something fresh."

"Such a good fellow, too," remarked the Otter. "But no stability—especially in a boat!"

From where they sat they could get a glimpse of the main stream across the island that separated them; and just then a wager-boat flashed into view, the rower—a short stout figure—splashing badly and rolling a good deal, but working his hardest. The Rat stood up and hailed him, but Toad —for it was he—shook his head and settled sternly to his work.

"He'll be out of the boat in a minute," said the Rat, sitting down again.

"Of course he will," chuckled the Otter. "Did I ever tell you that story. . . ."

A Mayfly swerved athwart the current.
A swirl of water and a "cloop!" and
the Mayfly was visible no more.

Neither was the Otter.

Again there was a streak of
bubbles on the surface of the river.

"Well," the Rat said. "I suppose we ought to be moving on.
I wonder which of us had better pack the luncheon-basket?"

"O, let me," said the Mole. So, of course, the Rat let him.

Packing the basket was not quite such pleasant work as
unpacking the basket. It never is. But the Mole was bent on
enjoying everything, and although just when he had got the job
done he saw a plate staring up at him from the grass, and then a
fork which anybody ought to have seen, and last of all the
mustard-pot—still, somehow, the thing got finished at last,
without much loss of temper.

The afternoon sun was getting low as the Rat sculled gently homewards, murmuring poetry things, and not paying much attention to Mole. But the Mole was full of lunch, and self-satisfaction, and pride, and already quite at home in a boat (so he thought) and presently he said, "Ratty! Please, *I* want to row!"

The Rat shook his head with a smile. "Not yet," he said. "Wait till you've had a few lessons. It's not so easy as it looks."

The Mole began to feel more and more jealous of Rat, sculling so strongly and easily along. His pride began to whisper he could do it every bit as well, and after a minute or two he suddenly jumped up and seized the sculls. The Rat, who was gazing out over the water, was taken by surprise. He fell backwards off his seat with his legs in the air for the second time, while the triumphant Mole took his place.

"Stop it, you *silly* ass!" cried the Rat from the bottom of the boat. "You'll have us over!"

The Mole flung his sculls back with a flourish and made a great dig at the water. He missed the surface altogether, his legs flew up above his head, and he found himself lying on top of the Rat. He made a grab at the side of the boat and the next moment—Sploosh!

Over went the boat, and he found himself struggling in the water.

O my, how cold the water was, and O, how *very* wet it felt. How it sang in his ears as he went down, down, down! How bright and welcome the sun looked as he rose to the surface. How black was his despair when he found himself sinking again! Then a firm paw gripped him by the back of his neck. It was the Rat, and he was laughing—the Mole could *feel* him laughing, right down his arm and through his paw.

The Rat got hold of a scull and shoved it under the Mole's arm, then he did the same by the other side of him and, swimming behind, propelled him to shore.

The Mole sat on the bank, a squashy lump of misery. When the Rat had rubbed him down a bit, and wrung some of the wet out of him, he said, "Now then, old fellow! Trot up and down the towing-path till you're dry, while I dive for the luncheon-basket."

So the dismal Mole, wet without and ashamed within, trotted about while the Rat plunged into the water again, righted the boat, fetched his floating property and finally dived for the luncheon-basket.

When all was ready the Mole, limp and dejected, took his seat in the stern of the boat. "Ratty!" he said as they set off, in a voice broken with emotion, "I am very sorry. I've been a complete ass, and I know it. To think I might have lost that beautiful luncheon-basket. Will you overlook it this once and let things go on as before?"

"That's all right," said Rat cheerily. "What's a little wet to a Water Rat? I'm more in the water than out of it most days. Don't you think any more about it; look here! I think you had better come and stop with me for a time. I'll teach you to row and swim and you'll soon be as handy on the water as any of us."

The Mole was so touched by his kind manner he could find no voice to answer him; and he had to brush away a tear or two with the back of his paw. But the Rat kindly looked in another direction and soon the Mole's spirits revived and he was even able to give some back-talk to a couple of moorhens who were sniggering to each other about his bedraggled appearance.

When they got home, the Rat made a bright fire in the parlour, and planted the Mole in an arm-chair, in front of it, in dressing gown and slippers, and told him river stories until supper-time. Very thrilling stories they were, too, to an earth-dwelling animal like Mole. Stories about weirs and sudden floods, leaping pike, and herons, adventures down drains and night-fishings with Otter, or excursions far afield with Badger.

Supper was a cheerful meal, but shortly afterwards a terribly sleepy Mole had to be escorted upstairs to the best bedroom, where he laid his head on his pillow in great peace and contentment, knowing that his new-found friend, the River, was lapping the sill of his window.

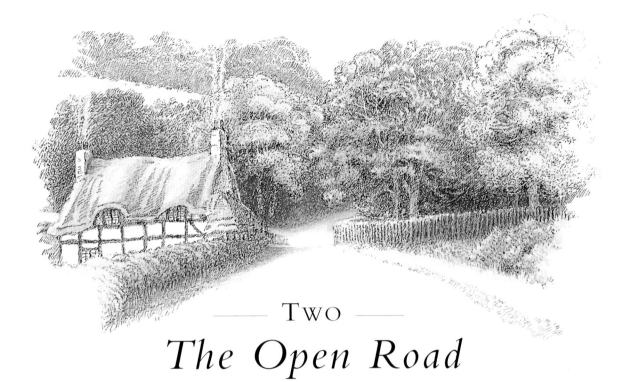

## —— Two ——
# *The Open Road*

"Ratty," said the Mole suddenly, one bright summer morning. "Please, I want to ask you a favour."

The Rat was sitting on the river bank, singing a little song he had just composed about ducks, which he called

### Duck's Ditty

*All along the backwater,*
*Through the rushes tall,*
*Ducks are a-dabbling,*
*Up tails all!*

*Ducks' tails, drakes' tails,*
*Yellow feet a-quiver,*
*Yellow bills all out of sight*
*Busy in the river!*

*Everyone for what he likes!*
*We like to be*
*Heads down, tails up,*
*Dabbling free!*

"I don't know that I think so *very* much of that little song, Rat," observed the Mole. He was no poet himself and didn't care who knew it. "But what I wanted to ask you was, won't you take me to call on Mr Toad?"

"Why, certainly," said the Rat, jumping to his feet. "Get the boat out at once. It's never the wrong time to call on Toad. He's always glad to see you, always sorry when you go!"

"He must be a very nice animal," observed the Mole, as he got into the boat and took the sculls.

"He is the best of animals," replied Rat. "Perhaps he's not very clever and it may be that he is boastful and conceited. But he has some great qualities, has Toady."

Rounding a bend in the river, they came in sight of Toad Hall, a handsome, dignified old house of mellowed red brick with well-kept lawns reaching down to the water's edge.

They left the boat in the boat-house, and went to look up Toad, whom they happened upon in a wicker garden-chair, a large map spread out on his knees.

"Hooray!" he cried, jumping up. "This is splendid!" He shook their paws. "How *kind* of you! I was just going to send a boat down the river for you, Ratty. I want you badly—both of you."

"It's about your rowing, I suppose," said the Rat. "You're getting on fairly well, and with coaching—"

"O, pooh! boating!" interrupted the Toad. "I've given that up *long* ago. No, I've discovered the real thing! Come with me and you shall see what you shall see!"

He led the way to the stable-yard and there, drawn out of the coach-house, they saw a gipsy caravan, shining with newness, painted a canary-yellow picked out with green, and red wheels.

"There you are!" cried the Toad, straddling and expanding himself. "There's real life for you. The open road, the dusty highway, the heath, the common, the rolling downs! Here today, and off somewhere else tomorrow! The whole world before you! And mind, this is the finest cart of its sort ever built."

The Mole followed him eagerly up the steps and into the caravan. It was very compact and comfortable. Little sleeping-bunks—a table that folded up against the wall—a cooking-stove, lockers, bookshelves and pots, pans, jugs and kettles of every size and variety.

"You see—" said the Toad, pulling open a locker, "biscuits, potted lobster, sardines—everything you can possibly want. Soda-water here—letter-paper there, bacon, jam, cards and dominoes—you'll find," he continued, "that nothing has been forgotten, when we make our start this afternoon."

"I beg your pardon," said the Rat, "but did I hear you say 'we,' and 'start,' and 'this afternoon'?"

"Dear Ratty," said Toad, "you've *got* to come. I can't manage without you. You don't mean to stick to your river all your life."

"I *am* going to stick to my river," said the Rat. "And what's more, Mole's going to stick to me, aren't you, Mole?"

"I'll always stick to you, Rat," said the Mole loyally. "All the same, it sounds as if it might have been—well, fun!" Poor Mole! He had fallen in love at first sight with the canary-coloured cart and all its little fitments.

The Rat saw what was in his mind and wavered. He was fond of the Mole, and would do almost anything to oblige him. Toad was watching them closely.

"Come along in and have some lunch," he said, "and we'll talk it over. We needn't decide anything in a hurry."

During lunch the Toad simply let himself go, painting the joys of the open life and roadside in such glowing colours that the Mole could hardly sit in his chair for excitement. Somehow, it seemed taken for granted that the trip was a settled thing; and the good-natured Rat could not bear to disappoint his two friends, who were already planning each day for several weeks ahead. The triumphant Toad led his companions to the paddock, and set them to capture the old grey horse, who, to his extreme annoyance, had been told off by Toad for the dustiest job in this expedition. He frankly preferred the paddock, and took a deal of catching. At last he was caught and harnessed and they set off, all talking at once, each animal either trudging by the side of the cart or sitting on the shaft, as the humour took him. It was a golden afternoon. The smell of the dust they kicked up was rich and satisfying; out of orchards on either side the road, birds called and whistled to them cheerily; wayfarers, passing them, gave them "Good day," or stopped to say nice things about their beautiful cart; and rabbits, sitting at their front doors in the hedgerows, held up their fore-paws, and said, "O my!"

Late in the evening, tired and happy and miles from home, they drew up on a remote common, turned the horse loose to graze, and ate their supper sitting on the grass by the side of the cart. Toad talked big about all he was going to do in the days to come, while stars grew fuller all around them . . .

and a yellow moon, appearing from nowhere in particular,

came to keep them company and listen to their talk.

At last they turned into their little bunks; and Toad, kicking out his legs, sleepily said, "Well, good night, you fellows! This is the life! Talk about your old river!"

"I *don't* talk about my river," replied the Rat. "You *know* I don't, Toad. But I *think* about it," he added. "I *think* about it all the time!" The Mole reached out from under his blanket, felt for the Rat's paw in the darkness, and gave it a squeeze. "Shall we run away tomorrow," he whispered, "—*very* early—and go back to our dear old hole on the river?"

"No, we'll see it out," whispered back the Rat. "I ought to stick by Toad till this trip is ended. It wouldn't be safe for him to be left to himself. It won't take very long. His fads never do."

The end was nearer than even the Rat suspected.

The Toad slept very soundly, and no amount of shaking could rouse him out of bed next morning. So the Mole and Rat turned to, and while the Rat saw to the horse, and lit a fire, and got things ready for breakfast, the Mole trudged off to the nearest village, a long way off, for milk and eggs, which the Toad had, of course, forgotten. The two animals were thoroughly exhausted by the time Toad appeared, fresh and gay, remarking what a pleasant easy life they were leading now, after the cares and worries of housekeeping at home.

They had a pleasant ramble that day over grassy downs, and camped, as before, on a common, only this time the guests took care that Toad should do his share of the work. Next morning their way lay across country by narrow lanes, and it was not till the afternoon that they came out on their first high road; and there disaster sprang out on them.

They were strolling along, the Mole by the horse's head, since the horse had complained that he was being left out of it; the Toad and the Water Rat walking behind the cart talking— at least Toad was talking, and Rat was saying at intervals, "Yes, and what did *you* say to *him*?"—and thinking all the time of something very different, when behind them they heard a warning hum, like the drone of a bee. Glancing back, they saw a small cloud of dust, with a dark centre of energy, advancing on them at incredible speed, while from out of the dust wailed a faint "Poop-poop!"

In an instant the peaceful scene was changed. The "poop-poop" rang with a brazen shout in their ears, and with a blast of wind and a whirl of sound that made them jump for the nearest ditch, the motor-car—its pilot tense and hugging his wheel—was on them. It flung a cloud of dust that blinded them utterly, and then dwindled to a speck in the far distance.

The old grey horse, rearing, plunging, backing steadily, in spite of all the Mole's efforts at his head, drove the cart backwards towards the side of the road. It wavered—then there was a heart-rending crash—and the canary-coloured cart lay on its side in a deep ditch.

"You villains!" shouted the Rat, shaking both fists. "You scoundrels, you—you—road-hogs!"

Toad sat in the middle of the road, his legs stretched out before him, his eyes fixed on the dusty wake of the motor-car. He breathed short, and at intervals murmured "Poop-poop!"

The Mole was trying to quiet the horse. The Rat came to help him. "Hi, Toad!" they cried. "Bear a hand, can't you!"

The Toad never budged. He was in a sort of trance, a happy smile on his face. "The *real* way to travel!" he murmured. "The *only* way to travel! O bliss! O poop-poop! And to think I never *knew*, never even *dreamt*! But *now*—now I know! What dust-clouds shall spring up behind me as I speed on my way! What carts I shall fling into the ditch! Horrid carts—common carts—canary-coloured carts!"

"What are we to do with him?" asked the Mole.

"Nothing," replied the Rat. "You see, I know him of old. He has got a new craze and it always takes him that way, like an animal in a happy dream, quite useless. Never mind him. Let's see about the cart."

FT 627

A careful inspection showed them that the cart would travel no longer. The axles were in a hopeless state, and one wheel was shattered into pieces.

The Rat took the horse by the head. "Come on!" he said to the Mole. "We shall just have to walk to the nearest town."

"But what about Toad?" asked the Mole.

"O, *bother* Toad," said the Rat.

They had not proceeded very far, however, when there was a pattering of feet behind them, and Toad caught them up.

"Now, look here, Toad!" said the Rat: "as soon as we get to the town, you'll go straight to the police-station, and lodge a complaint against that motor-car."

"Complaint! Me *complain* of that beautiful, heavenly vision! That swan, that sunbeam, that thunderbolt!"

The Rat turned from him in despair. "I give up," he said.

On reaching the town they went straight to the station and deposited Toad in the second-class waiting-room, giving a porter twopence to keep a strict eye on him. They left the horse at an inn stable, and gave what directions they could about the cart. Eventually, a slow train having landed them not far from Toad Hall, they escorted the spellbound Toad to his door. Then they got out their boat and sculled down the river, and at a very late hour sat down to supper in their own cosy parlour.

The following evening the Mole, who had taken things easy all day, was sitting on the bank fishing, when the Rat came strolling along to find him. "Heard the news?" he said. "There's nothing else being talked about, all along the river bank. Toad went up to Town by an early train this morning. And he has ordered a large and very expensive motor-car."

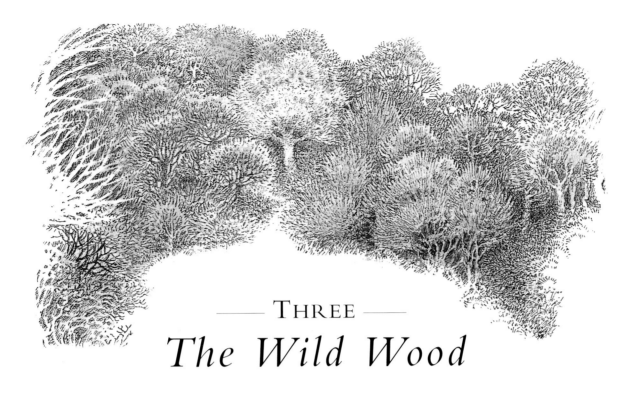

# THREE

# *The Wild Wood*

The Mole had long wanted to make the acquaintance of the Badger. But whenever he mentioned his wish to the Water Rat he always found himself put off. "Badger'll turn up some day," the Rat would say.

"Couldn't you ask him here—dinner or something?" said the Mole.

"He wouldn't come," replied the Rat simply. "Badger hates Society, and invitations, and dinner, and all that sort of thing."

"Well, supposing we call on *him*?" suggested the Mole.

"O, I'm sure he wouldn't like that at *all*," said the Rat. "He's so very shy. He'll be along some day."

But he never came along, and it was not till summer was over, and cold and frost kept them indoors, that the Mole found his thoughts dwelling again on the grey Badger.

And one cold still afternoon with a hard steely sky overhead, he slipped out of the warm parlour and went by himself to the Wild Wood, where Mr Badger lived.

There was nothing
to alarm him at first entry.
Twigs crackled under his feet, logs
tripped him, funguses on stumps startled him;
but that was all fun, and exciting. It led him on, to
where the light was less, and trees crouched nearer and
nearer, and holes made ugly mouths at him on either side.

Everything was very still now; and the light seemed to be draining away like flood-water.

Then the faces began.

It was over his shoulder that he first thought he saw a face: a little evil wedge-shaped face, looking out at him from a hole. When he turned the thing had vanished.

He quickened his pace, telling himself cheerfully not to begin imagining things, or there would be simply no end to it. He passed another hole, and another; then—yes!—no!—yes! a little narrow face, with hard eyes, had flashed up for an instant and was gone. He braced himself and strode on. Then suddenly, every hole, far and near, seemed to possess its face, all fixing on him glances of malice and hatred: all hard-eyed and evil and sharp.

If he could only get away from the holes in the banks, he thought, there would be no more faces. He swung off the path and plunged into the untrodden places of the wood.

Then the whistling began.

Very faint and shrill it was,
when first he heard it;
it made him hurry forward.
Then it sounded far ahead of him,
and made him want to go back.
As he halted it broke out on either side,
and passed throughout the whole length of the wood.
They were up and ready, whoever they were! And he—he was
alone, and unarmed, and far from help;
and the night was closing in.

Then the pattering began.

He thought it was only
falling leaves at first, so
slight was the sound
of it. Then as it grew
it took a rhythm,
and he knew it
for the pat-pat-
pat of little feet.
As he listened anxiously,
leaning this way and that,
it seemed to be closing in on him.
A rabbit came running towards him.
"Get out of this, you fool, get out!" the
Mole heard him mutter as he swung round
a stump and disappeared down a burrow.

The pattering increased till it sounded
like hail on the dry-leaf carpet spread
around him. The whole wood
seemed to be running now,
running hard, hunting,
chasing something
or—somebody?

In panic, he began to run too. He ran up against things.

He fell over things

and into things.

He darted under things and

dodged round things.

At last he took refuge in the dark hollow of an old beech tree. He was too tired to run any further, and could only snuggle down into the dry leaves and hope he was safe for the time. As he lay panting and trembling, and listened to the whistlings and patterings outside, he knew that dread thing which other little dwellers in field and hedgerow had encountered here and known as their darkest moment—the Terror of the Wild Wood!

Meantime the Rat dozed by his fireside. His paper of half-finished verses slipped from his knee, his head fell back and his mouth opened. Then a coal slipped. The fire crackled and he woke with a start. He reached down to the floor for his verses, pored over them for a minute, and then looked round for the Mole to ask him if he knew a good rhyme for something or other.

But the Mole was not there. He listened for a time. The house seemed very quiet.

Then he called "Moly!," got up and went out into the hall. The Mole's cap was missing from its accustomed peg. His goloshes, which always lay by the umbrella-stand, were also gone.

The Rat left the house and examined the muddy ground outside, hoping to find the Mole's tracks. There they were, sure enough. The goloshes were new, just bought for the winter, and the pimples on their soles were fresh and sharp. He could see the imprints of them in the mud, running along straight and purposeful, leading direct to the Wild Wood.

The Rat looked very grave. Then he re-entered the house, strapped a belt round his waist, shoved a brace of pistols into it, took up a stout cudgel that stood in a corner of the hall, and set off for the Wild Wood at a smart pace.

It was already getting towards dusk when he reached the first fringe of trees and plunged without hesitation into the wood, looking anxiously for any sign of his friend. Wicked little faces popped out of holes, but vanished at sight of the Rat, his pistols, and the great ugly cudgel in his grasp; and the whistling and pattering, which he had heard plainly on entry, died away, and all was still. He made his way through the length of the wood, calling cheerfully, "Moly! Where are you? It's me—Rat!"

He had hunted for an hour or more, when he heard a little answering cry. From out of the hole of an old beech tree came a feeble voice, saying, "Ratty! Is that really you?"

The Rat crept into the hollow, and there he found the Mole, exhausted and still trembling. "O Rat!" he cried, "I've been so frightened, you can't think!"

"You shouldn't really have gone and done it, Mole," said the Rat. "We river-bankers hardly ever come here by ourselves. If we have to come, we come in couples; then we're all right. Besides, there are a hundred things to know—passwords, and signs, and plants you carry in your pocket, and verses you repeat, and dodges and tricks; all simple enough when you know them, but they've got to be known if you're small, or you'll find yourself in trouble."

"Surely brave Mr Toad wouldn't mind coming here by himself, would he?" inquired the Mole.

"Old Toad?" said the Rat, laughing heartily. "He wouldn't show his face here for a hatful of guineas."

The Mole was cheered by the sound of the Rat's laughter, as well as by the sight of his stick and his gleaming pistols, and he stopped shivering and began to feel himself again.

"Now then," said the Rat, "we really must make a start for home. It will never do to spend the night here."

"Dear Ratty," said the poor Mole, "I'm simply dead beat. Let me rest a while longer, and get my strength back."

"O, all right," said the Rat. "It's nearly dark now, anyhow; and there ought to be a bit of a moon later."

So the Mole got well into the dry leaves and stretched out, and dropped off into sleep; while the Rat covered himself up for warmth, and lay waiting, with a pistol in his paw.

When at last the Mole woke refreshed and in his usual spirits, the Rat said, "I'll just see if everything's quiet."

He went to the entrance of their retreat and put his head out. Then the Mole heard him saying to himself, "Hullo! hullo! here —*is*—a—go!"

"What's up, Ratty?" asked the Mole.

"*Snow* is up," replied the Rat; "or *down*. It's snowing hard."

The Mole, looking out, saw the wood quite changed. Holes, pitfalls, and other black menaces were vanishing fast, and a gleaming carpet of faery was springing up everywhere.

"Well, it can't be helped," said the Rat. "We must make a start, I suppose. The worst of it is, I don't exactly know where we are. And this snow makes everything look so very different."

It did indeed. The Mole would not have known that it was the same wood. However, they set out bravely, and took the line that seemed most promising.

An hour or two later they pulled up, weary, and hopelessly at sea, and sat down on a fallen tree-trunk. They were aching, and bruised with tumbles; they had fallen into several holes and got wet through; the snow was getting so deep they could hardly drag their little legs through it. There seemed to be no end to this wood, and no beginning, and no difference in it, and, worst of all, no way out.

"We can't sit here," said the Rat. "We shall have to make another push for it. There's a sort of dell down there, where the ground seems all hilly and hummocky. We'll make our way down into that, and try and find some sort of shelter, and we'll have a rest before we try again. Besides, the snow may leave off, or something may turn up."

So they got on their feet, and struggled down into the dell, where they hunted about for a cave or corner that was a protection from the keen wind and the whirling snow, when suddenly the Mole tripped up and fell forward on his face with a squeal.

"O, my leg!" he cried. "O, my poor shin!" and he sat up on the snow and nursed his leg in both his front paws.

"Poor old Mole!" said the Rat kindly. "You don't seem to be having much luck today, do you?"

"I must have tripped over a hidden branch or a stump," said the Mole miserably. "O my! O my!"

"It's a very clean cut," said the Rat, examining it. "That was never done by a branch or a stump. Looks as if it was made by a sharp edge of something metal. Funny!"

"Well, never mind what done it," said the Mole, forgetting his grammar in his pain. "It hurts, whatever done it."

But the Rat, after tying up the leg with his handkerchief, was scraping in the snow.

Suddenly he cried, "Hooray! Hooray-oo-ray-oo-ray-oo-ray!" and executed a feeble jig.

"What *have* you found, Ratty?" asked the Mole, hobbling up.

"A door-scraper! Why dance jigs round a door-scraper?"

"But don't you see what it *means,* you—you dull-witted animal?" cried the Rat impatiently.

"Of course I see what it means," replied the Mole. "It means that some *very* careless and forgetful person has left his door-scraper lying about in the middle of the Wild Wood, *just* where it's *sure* to trip *everybody* up!"

"O dear! O dear!" cried the Rat, in despair. "Here, stop arguing and come and scrape!"

After some further efforts, a very shabby door-mat lay exposed to view.

"What did I tell you?" exclaimed the Rat in great triumph.

"Nothing," replied the Mole, with perfect truthfulness. "You seem to have found another piece of domestic litter. Better dance your jig round that, and get it over, then perhaps we can go and not waste any more time over rubbish-heaps. Can we *eat* a door-mat? Or sleep under a door-mat? Or sit on a door-mat and sledge home on it?"

"Do—you—mean—to—say," cried the excited Rat, "that this door-mat doesn't *tell* you anything?"

"Really, Rat," said the Mole pettishly. "Who ever heard of a door-mat *telling* anyone anything? They simply don't do it. They are not that sort at all."

"Now look here, you—you thick-headed beast," replied the Rat, really angry, "this must stop. Not another word. Scrape, scratch and dig, if you want to sleep dry and warm tonight."

The Rat attacked a snow-bank, probing with his cudgel everywhere and digging with fury; and the Mole scraped busily too, more to oblige the Rat than for any other reason, for his opinion was that his friend was getting light-headed.

Some ten minutes' hard work, and the point of Rat's cudgel struck something hollow. He called the Mole to come and help him. Hard at it went the two animals, till at last in the side of what had seemed to be a snow-bank stood a solid-looking little door, painted a dark green. An iron bell-pull hung by the side, and below it, on a small brass plate neatly engraved in square capital letters, they read:

# MR BADGER

The Mole fell backwards on the snow from sheer surprise. "Rat!" he cried, "you're a wonder! A real wonder, that's what you are. I see it all now! You argued it out, step by step, in that wise head of yours, from the moment I fell and cut my shin, and you looked at the cut, and your majestic mind said, 'Door-scraper!' And then you found the door-scraper. Did you stop there? No. Some people would have been quite satisfied; but not you. 'Let me find a door-mat,' says you to yourself. And of course you found your door-mat. You're so clever, I believe you could find anything you liked. 'Now to find that door!' says you. Well, I've read about that sort of thing in books, but I've never come across it in real life. You're simply wasted here, among us fellows. If I only had your head, Ratty—"

"But as you haven't," interrupted the Rat rather unkindly, "I suppose you're going to sit on the snow all night and *talk*? Get up and hang on to that bell-pull, and ring as hard as you can, while I hammer!"

While the Rat attacked the door with his stick, the Mole sprang up at the bell-pull, clutched it and swung there, both feet well off the ground, and from quite a long way off they could faintly hear a deep-toned bell respond.

## —— FOUR ——

# *Mr Badger*

They waited patiently for what seemed a very long time, stamping in the snow to keep their feet warm. At last they heard the sound of slow shuffling footsteps approaching the door from the inside. It seemed, as the Mole remarked to the Rat, like someone walking in carpet slippers that were too large for him and down-at-heel; which was intelligent of Mole, because that was exactly what it was.

There was the noise of a bolt shot back, and the door opened a few inches, to show a long snout and a pair of sleepy eyes.

"Now, the *very* next time this happens," said a gruff and suspicious voice, "I shall be exceedingly angry. Who is it *this* time, disturbing people on such a night? Speak up!"

"O, Badger," cried the Rat, "let us in, please. It's me, Rat, and my friend Mole, and we've lost our way in the snow."

"Ratty!" exclaimed the Badger, in quite a different voice. "Come along in, both of you. Why, you must be perished. Well, I never! Lost in the snow! And in the Wild Wood too, at this time of night!"

The two animals tumbled over each other in their eagerness to get inside, and heard the door shut behind them with great joy and relief. The Badger, who wore a long dressing-gown, and whose slippers were indeed very down-at-heel, carried a flat candlestick and had probably been on his way to bed when their summons sounded. "This is not the sort of night for small animals to be out," he said. "I'm afraid you've been up to some of your pranks again, Ratty."

He shuffled on in front of them, carrying the light, and they followed him down a long, and to tell the truth, decidedly shabby passage, into a sort of a hall, out of which they could see other passages branching mysteriously. There were doors as well—stout oaken doors. One of these the Badger flung open, and they found themselves in all the glow and warmth of a large fire-lit kitchen.

The kindly Badger thrust them down on a settle to toast themselves at the fire, and bade them remove their wet coats and boots. Then he fetched them dressing-gowns and slippers, and bathed the Mole's shin with warm water and mended the cut with sticking-plaster till the whole thing was as good as new, if not better. Warm and dry at last, with weary legs propped up in front of them, it seemed to the storm-driven animals that the cold and trackless Wild Wood just left outside was miles and miles away, and all that they had suffered in it a half-forgotten dream.

When at last they were thoroughly toasted, the Badger summoned them to the table. They had felt pretty hungry before, but when they saw the supper spread for them, it seemed only a question of what they should attack first where all was so attractive, and whether the other things would wait till they had time to give them attention. Conversation was impossible for a long time; and when it was resumed, it was that regrettable sort that results from talking with your mouth full. The Badger did not mind that sort of thing at all, nor did he take any notice of elbows on the table, or everybody speaking at once. As the animals told their story, he did not seem surprised or shocked at anything. He never said, "I told you so," or, "Just what I always said," or remarked that they ought to have done so-and-so, or ought not to have done something else. The Mole began to feel very friendly towards him.

Supper finished, they gathered round the glowing embers of the great fire, and thought how jolly it was to be sitting up *so* late, and *so* full; and after they had chatted for a time, the Badger said, "Well, it's time we were all in bed." He conducted the two animals to a long room that seemed half bedchamber and half loft. The Badger's winter stores took up half the room, but the two little beds on the remainder of the floor looked soft and inviting, and the linen on them, though coarse, was clean and smelt beautifully of lavender; and the Mole and the Water Rat, shaking off their garments in some thirty seconds, tumbled in between the sheets in great joy and contentment.

The two tired animals
came down to breakfast
very late next morning,
and found a bright fire
burning in the kitchen,
and two young
hedgehogs sitting
on a bench at
the table, eating
oatmeal porridge
out of wooden
bowls.

The hedgehogs dropped their spoons and rose to their feet respectfully as the two entered.

"Sit down, sit down," said the Rat pleasantly, "and go on with your porridge. Where have you youngsters come from? Lost your way in the snow, I suppose?"

"Yes, please, sir," said the elder of the two hedgehogs. "Me and Billy was trying to find our way to school and we lost ourselves, sir, and Billy got frightened and took and cried, being young. And we happened up against Mr Badger's back door, and knocked, sir, for Mr Badger he's a kind-hearted gentleman, as everyone knows—"

"I understand," said the Rat, cutting himself some rashers of bacon, while the Mole dropped some eggs into a saucepan. "And what's the weather like outside? You needn't 'sir' me quite so much," he added.

"O, terrible bad, sir, terrible deep the snow is," said the hedgehog. "No getting out for you gentlemen today."

"Where's Mr Badger?" inquired the Mole.

"The master's gone into his study, sir," replied the hedgehog, "and said as how he was going to be particular busy this morning, and on no account was he to be disturbed."

The animals well knew that Badger, having eaten a hearty breakfast, had retired to his study and settled himself in an armchair with his legs on another and a red cotton handkerchief over his face, and was being "busy" in the usual way at this time of the year.

The front-door bell clanged loudly, and the Rat, who was very greasy with buttered toast, sent Billy, the smaller hedge-hog, to see who it might be. There was a sound of much stamping in the hall, and presently Billy returned in front of the Otter, who threw himself on the Rat with a shout.

"Get off!" spluttered the Rat, with his mouth full.

"Thought I should find you here," said the Otter cheerfully. "They were all in a state along River Bank this morning. Rat never been home all night—nor Mole either—something dreadful must have happened, they said; and the snow had covered your tracks. But I knew when people were in any fix they mostly went to Badger, so I came straight here, through the Wild Wood. About halfway across I came on a rabbit sitting on a stump, cleaning his silly face. I managed to extract from him that Mole had been seen in the Wild Wood last night. It was the talk of the burrows, he said, how Mole, Mr Rat's particular friend, was in a bad fix; how he had lost his way, and 'They' were up and out hunting, and were chivvying him round and round. 'Why didn't you *do* something?' I asked. 'What, us?' he said: '*do* something? us rabbits?' So I cuffed him. There was nothing else to be done. At any rate, I had learnt something; and if I had had the luck to meet 'Them' I'd have learnt something more—or *they* would."

"Weren't you—er—nervous?" asked the Mole.

"Nervous?" The Otter laughed. "I'd give 'em nerves if any of them tried anything on with me. Here, Mole, fry me some slices of ham. I'm hungry, and I've any amount to say to Ratty here. Haven't seen him for an age."

So the good-natured Mole, having cut some slices of ham, set the hedgehogs to fry it, and returned to his own breakfast, while the Otter and the Rat talked river-shop.

A plate of fried ham had just been cleared and sent back for more, when the Badger entered, yawning and rubbing his eyes, and greeted them. "It must be getting on for luncheon time," he remarked to the Otter. "Better stop and have it with us. You must be hungry, this cold morning."

"Rather!" replied the Otter, winking at the Mole.

The hedgehogs, who were just beginning to feel hungry again after working so hard at their frying, looked timidly up at Mr Badger, but were too shy to say anything.

"You be off to your mother," said the Badger kindly. "I'll send someone with you to show you the way."

He gave them sixpence apiece and they went off.

Presently they all sat down to luncheon together. The Mole found himself next to Mr Badger, and, as the other two were still deep in river-gossip, he took the opportunity to tell Badger how home-like it all felt to him. "Once underground," he said, "you know exactly where you are. Nothing can happen to you, and nothing can get at you. Things go on all the same overhead, and you don't bother about 'em. When you want to, up you go, and there the things are, waiting for you."

The Badger beamed on him. "That's exactly what I say," he replied. "There's no security, or peace, except underground. Look at Rat, now. A couple of feet of flood-water, and he's got  to move into hired lodgings. Take Toad. I say nothing against Toad Hall; quite the best house in these parts, *as* a house. But supposing a fire breaks out—where's Toad? Supposing tiles are blown off, or windows get broken—where's Toad? No, up and out of doors is good enough to roam about and get one's living in; but underground—that's my idea of *home!*"

The Mole assented heartily; and the Badger got very friendly with him. "When lunch is over," he said, "I'll take you round this little place of mine."

Accordingly, when the other two had settled themselves into the chimney-corner and had started a heated argument on the subject of *eels,* the Badger lighted a lantern and bade the Mole follow him. Crossing the hall, they passed down one of the tunnels, and the wavering light gave glimpses on either side of rooms, some mere cupboards, others nearly as broad and imposing as Toad's dining-hall. A passage at right angles led into another corridor, and here the same thing was repeated. The Mole was staggered at the size of it all; at the length of the dim passages, the vaultings, the pillars, the arches.

71

"How on earth, Badger," said the Mole at last,

"did you do all this? It's astonishing!"

"It *would* be astonishing," said the Badger, "if I *had* done it. But as a matter of fact I did none of it—only cleaned out the passages, as I had need of them. You see, long ago, on the spot where the Wild Wood waves now, before ever it had planted itself and grown, there was a city—a city of people, you know. Here, where we are standing, they walked, and talked, and carried on their business. They were a powerful people, and rich, and great builders."

"But what has become of them all?" asked the Mole.

"Who can tell?" said the Badger. "People come—they stay for a while—and they go. But we remain. There were badgers here long before that same city ever came to be. And now there are badgers here again."

When they got back to the kitchen again, they found the Rat very restless. The underground atmosphere was getting on his nerves, and he seemed to be afraid that the river would run away if he wasn't there to look after it. He had his overcoat on, and his pistols thrust into his belt again. "Come along, Mole," he said. "We must get off while it's light. Don't want to spend another night in the Wild Wood."

"It'll be all right," said the Otter. "I'm coming with you. I know every path blindfold; and if there's a head to be punched, you can rely upon me to punch it."

"You needn't fret, Ratty," added the Badger. "My passages run further than you think, and I've bolt-holes to the edge of the wood in several directions, though I don't care for everybody to know about them. When you really have to go, you shall leave by one of my short cuts."

The Rat was still anxious to be off, so the Badger, taking up his lantern again, led the way along a damp and airless tunnel that wound and dipped for what seemed to be miles. At last daylight began to show itself through tangled growth overhanging the mouth of the passage; and the Badger, bidding them a hasty good-bye, pushed them through, made everything look as natural as possible again, with brushwood, and dead leaves, and retreated.

They found themselves standing on the very edge of the Wild Wood. Rocks and brambles and tree-roots behind them; in front, a great space of fields, hemmed by lines of hedges black on the snow, and, far ahead, a glint of the familiar old river, while the wintry sun hung red and low on the horizon. They trailed out on a bee-line for a distant stile. Pausing there and looking back, they saw the whole of the Wild Wood, menacing, compact, grimly set in vast white surroundings; they turned and made for home, for firelight and the familiar things it played on, for the voice of the river they knew and trusted, that never made them afraid.

As he hurried along, the Mole saw clearly he was an animal of field and hedgerow, the ploughed furrow, the frequented pasture, the lane of evening lingerings, the cultivated garden-plot. For others the conflict that went with Nature in the rough; he must be wise, must keep to the places in which his lines were laid and which held adventure enough, in their way, to last for a lifetime.

## — FIVE —

# *Dulce Domum*

The sheep ran huddling together against the hurdles, blowing out thin nostrils and stamping with delicate forefeet, their heads thrown back and a light steam rising from the crowded sheep-pen into the frosty air, as the two animals hastened by in high spirits. They were returning across country after a day's outing with Otter, and the shades of the short winter day were closing in. They had heard the sheep and had made for them; and now, leading from the sheep-pen, they found a beaten track.

"It looks as if we're coming to a village," said the Mole, slackening his pace.

"O, at this season of the year," said the Rat, "they're safe indoors by this time, men, women, children and all. We shall slip through without any bother."

The rapid nightfall of mid-December had quite beset the little village as they approached it on soft feet over a first thin fall of powdery snow. Little was visible but squares of a dusky orange-red on either side of the street, where the firelight or lamplight of each cottage overflowed through the casements into the dark world without. Most of the low latticed windows were innocent of blinds, and moving from one to another, the lookers-in, so far from home themselves, watched a cat being stroked, a sleepy child picked up and huddled off to bed, or a tired man stretch and knock out his pipe on the end of a smouldering log.

But it was from one little window, with its blind drawn down, that the sense of home most pulsated. Against the blind hung a bird-cage, clearly silhouetted. On the perch, the fluffy occupant, head tucked well into feathers, seemed so near to them as to be easily stroked, had they tried. As they looked, the sleepy little fellow stirred, shook himself, and raised his head. They could see the gape of his tiny beak as he yawned in a bored sort of way, looked around, and settled again. Then a gust of bitter wind took them in the back of the neck, a small sting of frozen sleet woke them as from a dream, and they knew their toes to be cold and their legs tired, and their own home distant a weary way.

Once beyond the village, they could smell the friendly fields again; and they braced themselves for the last long stretch, the home stretch, the stretch that we know is bound to end in the rattle of the door-latch, sudden firelight, and the sight of familiar things greeting us. They plodded along steadily and silently, each of them thinking his own thoughts. The Mole's ran a good deal on supper, as it was pitch dark, and it was all strange country to him as far as he knew. The Rat was walking a little way ahead, his eyes fixed on the road in front of him; so he did not notice Mole when the summons reached him, and took him like an electric shock.

We have only the word "smell" for the whole range of delicate thrills which murmur in the nose of the animal night and day. It was one of these mysterious fairy calls that suddenly reached Mole in the darkness, making him tingle through and through. He stopped dead in his tracks, his nose searching hither and thither.

Home! That was what they meant, those soft touches wafted through the air, those invisible little hands pulling and tugging, all one way! Why, it must be quite close by him at that moment, his old home he had forsaken when he first found the river! Since that bright morning he had hardly given it a thought. Shabby and poorly furnished, and yet his, the home he had made for himself, the home he had been so happy to get back to after his day's work. And the home was missing him, and wanted him back, and was telling him so, through his nose, sorrowfully, but with no bitterness or anger; that it was there, and wanted him.

"Ratty!" he called. "Come back! I want you, quick!"

"O, *come* along, Mole!" replied the Rat, plodding along.

"Stop, Ratty!" pleaded the Mole. "You don't understand! It's my home, my old home! I've just come across the smell of it, and it's really quite close. Come back, Ratty! Please!"

The Rat was by this time very far ahead, too far to hear what the Mole was calling.

"We mustn't stop now!" he called back. "It's late, and the snow's coming on again, and I'm not sure of the way! And I want your nose, Mole, so come on, there's a good fellow!" And the Rat pressed on without waiting for an answer.

Poor Mole stood alone in the road, his heart torn asunder, a big sob gathering, somewhere low down inside him. Never for a moment did he dream of abandoning his friend. His old home pleaded, whispered. With a wrench he followed in the track of the Rat, while faint, thin little smells, still dogging his nose, reproached him for his forgetfulness.

He caught up to the Rat, who began chattering about what they would do when they got back, and how jolly a fire in the parlour would be, and what a supper he meant to eat; never noticing his companion's silence. At last, when they were passing some tree-stumps at the edge of a copse, he stopped and said kindly, "Look here, Mole, old chap, you seem dead tired. No talk left in you, and your feet dragging like lead. We'll sit down here for a minute and rest. The snow has held off, and the best part of our journey is over."

The Mole tried to control himself, for he felt it coming, the sob he had fought so long. Up and up, it forced its way to the air, and then another, and another, and others thick and fast; till poor Mole at last gave up the struggle, and cried helplessly, now that he knew it was all over and he had lost what he could hardly be said to have found.

The Rat did not dare to speak for a while. At last he said, "What is it, old fellow? Whatever can be the matter?"

Mole found it difficult to get any words out. "I know it's a—shabby, little place," he sobbed at last: "not like—your cosy quarters—or Toad's beautiful hall—or Badger's great house—but it was my own little home—and I was fond of it—and then I smelt it suddenly—on the road, when I called and you wouldn't listen, Rat.—We might have just gone and had one look at it—but you wouldn't turn back, you wouldn't!"

The Rat stared in front of him, saying nothing. After a time he muttered, "What a *pig* I have been! A *pig*—that's me!"

Then he rose, and, remarking, "Well, we'd better be getting on!" set off up the road again, the way they had come.

"Wherever are you (hic) going to, Ratty?" cried the Mole.

"We're going to find that home of yours, old fellow," replied the Rat pleasantly.

"Come back, Ratty, do!" cried the Mole, hurrying after him. "The snow's coming! Think of River Bank, and your supper!"

"Hang River Bank!" said the Rat heartily.

When it seemed they must be nearing that part of the road where the Mole had been "held up," Rat said, "Now! Use your nose!"

Mole stood a moment rigid. His uplifted nose, quivering slightly, felt the air.

Then a short, quick run forward—a fault—a check—a try back; and then a slow, steady, confident advance.

The Rat kept close to his heels as the Mole, with something of the air of a sleep-walker, crossed a dry ditch, scrambled through a hedge, and nosed his way over a field open and trackless and bare in the faint starlight.

Suddenly he dived; the Rat promptly followed him down the tunnel to which his unerring nose had faithfully led him. It was close and airless, and the earthy smell was strong. The Mole struck a match, and by its light the Rat saw that they were standing in an open space, neatly swept and sanded underfoot, and directly facing them was Mole's little front door, with "Mole End" painted, in Gothic lettering, over the bell-pull at the side.

Mole reached down a lantern from a nail on the wall and lit it, and the Rat, looking round him, saw that they were in a sort of fore-court. A garden-seat stood on one side of the door, and on the other, a roller; for the Mole, who was a tidy animal, could not stand having his ground kicked up into earth-heaps. On the walls hung wire baskets with ferns in them, brackets carrying plaster statuary—Garibaldi, and the infant Samuel, and Queen Victoria, and other heroes of modern Italy. Down one side of the fore-court ran a skittle-alley, with benches along it and little wooden tables. In the middle was a small pond containing goldfish and surrounded by a cockle-shell border. Out of the centre of the pond rose a fanciful erection clothed in more cockle-shells and topped by a large silvered glass ball that reflected everything all wrong and had a very pleasing effect.

Mole's face beamed at the sight of all these objects so dear to him, and he hurried Rat through the door, lit a lamp in the hall, and took one glance round his old home. He saw the dust lying thick on everything, saw the cheerless, deserted look of the long-neglected house, and its worn and shabby contents—and collapsed again on a hall-chair, his nose in his paws.

"O, Ratty!" he cried dismally, "why ever did I do it? Why did I bring you to this poor, cold place, when you might have been at River Bank, with all your nice things about you!"

The Rat was running here and there, opening doors, and cupboards; lighting lamps and candles and sticking them up everywhere. "What a capital little house this is!" he called out cheerily. "We'll make a jolly night of it. The first thing we want is a good fire; I'll see to that. You get a duster, Mole, and try and smarten things up a bit."

Encouraged by his companion, the Mole roused himself and dusted with energy, while the Rat soon had a cheerful blaze roaring up the chimney. But Mole had another fit of the blues, dropping on a couch and burying his face in his duster.

"Rat," he moaned, "you poor, hungry, animal. I've nothing to give you—nothing—not a crumb!"

"What a fellow you are for giving in!" said the Rat. "Why, only just now I saw a sardine-opener on the kitchen dresser, quite distinctly; and everybody knows that means there are sardines about somewhere. Come with me and forage."

They went hunting through every cupboard and drawer. The result was not so depressing after all, though of course it might have been better; a tin of sardines—a box of captain's biscuits, nearly full—and a German sausage in silver paper.

The Rat busied himself fetching plates, knives and forks, and mustard which he mixed in an egg-cup, and had just got seriously to work with the sardine-opener when sounds were heard from the fore-court without—like the scuffling of small feet in the gravel and a murmur of tiny voices—"All in a line—hold the lantern up a bit, Tommy—no coughing after I say one, two, three.—Come on, we're all a-waiting—"

"What's up?" inquired the Rat.

"I think it must be the field-mice," replied the Mole, with a touch of pride in his manner. "They go round carol-singing regularly at this time of year. They're quite an institution in these parts. And they never pass me over—they come to Mole End last of all; and I used to give them hot drinks, and supper too sometimes, when I could afford it. It will be like old times to hear them again."

"Let's have a look at them!" cried the Rat, jumping up and running to the door.

In the fore-court, lit by the dim rays of a horn lantern, some eight or ten little field-mice stood in a semicircle, red worsted comforters round their throats, their fore-paws thrust deep into their pockets, their feet jigging for warmth. With bright beady eyes they glanced shyly at each other, sniggering a little, sniffing and applying coat-sleeves a good deal.

As the door opened, their shrill little voices uprose on the air.

## Carol

Villagers all, this frosty tide,
Let your doors swing open wide,
Though wind may follow,
    and snow beside,
Yet draw us in by your fire to bide;
Joy shall be yours in the morning!

Here we stand in the cold and sleet,
Blowing fingers and stamping feet,
Come from far away you to greet—
You by the fire and we in the street—
Bidding you joy in the morning!

"Well sung!" cried the Rat. "And now come along in, all of you, and have something hot!"

"Yes, come along, field-mice," cried the Mole eagerly. "You just wait a minute, while we—O, Ratty!" he cried in despair. "Whatever are we doing? We've nothing to give them!"

"You leave all that to me," said the Rat. "Here, you with the lantern! Are there any shops open at this hour of the night?"

"Certainly, sir," replied the field-mouse respectfully. "At this time of year our shops keep open to all sorts of hours."

"Then you go off at once," said the Rat, "and get me—" Here the Mole only heard "Fresh, mind!—no, a pound will do—only the best—if you can't get it there, try somewhere else— of course, home-made, no tinned stuff —well, do the best you can!" There was a chink of coin passing from paw to paw, the field-mouse was provided with a basket for his purchases, and off he hurried, he and his lantern.

The rest of the field-mice perched in a row on the settle, their small legs swinging.

"They act plays too," the Mole explained to the Rat. "Make them up all by themselves. They gave us a capital one last year, about a field-mouse who was captured at sea and made to row in a galley; and when he escaped and got home, his lady-love had gone into a convent. Here, you were in it, I remember. Get up and recite a bit."

The field-mouse addressed got up on his legs, giggled shyly, looked round the room, and remained absolutely tongue-tied. His comrades cheered him on, Mole coaxed him, but nothing could overcome his stage-fright. Then the door opened, and the field-mouse with the lantern reappeared, staggering under the weight of his basket.

In a few minutes supper was ready, and Mole, as he took the head of the table, saw his little friends' faces brighten and beam as they fell to and thought what a happy home-coming this had turned out, after all. As they ate, they talked of old times,

and the field-mice gave him the local gossip up to date, and answered as well as they could the hundred questions he had to ask them. The Rat said little or nothing, only taking care that each guest had what he wanted, and plenty of it, and that Mole had no trouble or anxiety about anything.

They clattered off at last, with their jacket pockets stuffed with remembrances for the small brothers and sisters at home. When the door had closed on the last of them and the chink of the lanterns had died away, Mole and Rat kicked the fire up, drew their chairs in, and discussed the events of the long day. At last the Rat, with a tremendous yawn, said, "Mole, old chap, I'm ready to drop. Sleepy is simply not the word. That your own bunk over on that side? Very well, then, I'll take this. What a ripping little house this is! Everything so handy!"

He clambered into his bunk and rolled himself well up in the blankets, and slumber gathered him forthwith.

The weary Mole also soon had his head on his pillow. But ere he closed his eyes he let them wander round his old room, mellow in the glow of the firelight that played on familiar and friendly things. He saw clearly how plain and simple—how narrow, even—it all was; but clearly, too, how much it all meant to him. He did not at all want to abandon the new life, to turn his back on sun and air; the upper world was all too strong, it called to him still, even down there, and he knew he must return. But it was good to think he had this to come back to, this place which was all his own, these things which were so glad to see him again and could always be counted upon for the same simple welcome.